ILLUMINATION PRESENTS

minions

Seek and Find Collection

Minions: Seek and Find originally published in May 2015 by Little, Brown and Company
Despicable Me 3: Seek and Find originally published in May 2017 by Little, Brown and Company

Cover design by Ching N. Chan. Cover illustration by Fractured Pixels.

Little, Brown and Company
Hachette Book Group
1290 Avenue of the Americas, New York, NY 10104
Visit us at LBYR.com

First Bindup Edition: June 2020

LB kids is an imprint of Little, Brown and Company.
The LB kids name and logo are trademarks of Hachette Book Group, Inc.

The publisher is not responsible for websites (or their content) that are not owned by the publisher.

ISBN: 978-0-316-53811-4

Printed in China

APS

10 9 8 7 6 5 4 3 2 1

LITTLE, BROWN & COMPANY
LB kids

The story of the Minions goes back to the dawn of time. They wandered the Earth for millions of years, looking to serve the most perfect, despicable master. Master after master, year after year, the Minions were left disappointed.

Then along came Gru.

Gru was the best master. He wanted to be the world's number one supervillain, and he planned to steal the moon.

Then Gru met Margo, Edith, and Alice. Forget villainy—now all Gru wanted to be was the world's number one dad.

It wasn't long until Gru met a super spy named Lucy. They fell in love and became determined to do their best as parents to the girls.

Throughout this book, you'll need to help seek and find everything from hidden treasure to weird animals to stuffed unicorns. Don't forget to keep an eye out for bananas. Minions *love* bananas.

Good luck!

Minions
Seek and Find

Written by Trey King

Art by Fractured Pixels

Based on the Motion Picture Screenplay by Brian Lynch

Prehistoric Beach Party!

Minions were some of the first creatures to walk the earth—which means they invented BBQs and pool parties! Check out these crafty and despicable Minion ancestors as they show the world how to have a good time.

CAN YOU SPOT:

DINOSAUR DINNERTIME!

Dinosaurs are massive creatures that roamed the earth millions of years ago. The only things bigger than their bodies were their appetites! It's time to eat, so the Minions are making a feast. Care to join them?

CAN YOU SPOT:

8

CAVEMAN HANGOUT!

Woolly mammoths! Saber-toothed tigers! Cavemen! Minions seem to know all the cool (prehistoric) people! Everyone is hanging out having a good time.

CAN YOU SPOT:

Building the pyramids was no easy task—good thing Minions were around to help out. With all these yellow helpers, the job should be done in no time—unless someone makes a mess of things....

CAN YOU SPOT:

Oh no! Those pirates are taking stuff. What a bunch of bullies. Pirates are well-known for stealing all sorts of things, like gold, precious gems, treasure, princesses, and...bananas?!

CAN YOU SPOT:

MARCH OF THE MINION ARMY!

At one point, Minions worked under the famous French military leader Napoleon. Sure, the Minions could have been fighting a battle, but instead, they chose to do things their way.

CAN YOU SPOT:

After so much hard work, Minions deserve a day off. What better way to spend it than building snowmen, snow-women, and snow-*Minions*?!

CAN YOU SPOT:

New York City Takeover!

This city is used to tourists from all over the world, but all these tourists look the same! Minions have taken over the City That Never Sleeps. I wonder what they're going to do first.

CAN YOU SPOT:

VILLAIN-CON!

If you're looking for a despicable new master (or just an evil friend to rob banks and toy stores with), then Villain-Con is the place to be. Just watch your wallet closely. In this crowd, it's likely to get stolen.

CAN YOU SPOT:

British Invasion!

In the mood for fish-and-chips and a spot of tea? Then the Minions have come to the right place. In London, there's lots of sightseeing, but right now, the neatest things to see are Minions!

CAN YOU SPOT:

The End? Nope!

We have a few more things hidden for you. Go back for another look and see if you can spot these extra-fun Minions and others things.

CAN YOU SPOT: 1 Minion wearing starfish

CAN YOU SPOT: 1 Minion in a barrel

CAN YOU SPOT: 1 Minion with a parachute

CAN YOU SPOT: 1 Minion with bunny ears

CAN YOU SPOT: 1 Minion cave painting

CAN YOU SPOT: 1 Minion driving a car

CAN YOU SPOT: 1 Minion with a croc-hunter hat

CAN YOU SPOT: 1 rocket ship ride

CAN YOU SPOT: 1 Minion with a sword in his mouth

CAN YOU SPOT: King Bob!

Seek and Find

Written by Trey King
Art by Fractured Pixels
Based on the Motion Picture Screenplay by
Cinco Paul and Ken Duario

FUN IN THE SUN!

Grucy (that means Gru *and* Lucy) just foiled Balthazar Bratt's plan to steal the world's largest diamond. Minions Jerry and Dave tried to help, but they got distracted—and started a dance party on the beach!

CAN YOU SPOT:

BAD DAY AT THE OFFICE

The AVL has a new boss in charge, and her name is Valerie Da Vinci! She does not like Gru, and decides to fire him. Lucy tries to help, and is fired, too.

CAN YOU SPOT:

SURPRISE HONEYMOON

When Gru and Lucy get home, the girls have a surprise planned for them. Since they never had a honeymoon, the girls made a tiki party in the backyard. They even made gummy-bear-and-meat soup. Yum?

CAN YOU SPOT:

MINIONS ON STRIKE!

Gru tells the Minions he lost his job. Mel and the other Minions are excited for their master to return to his evil ways—except Gru doesn't plan on doing that. Now Mel is organizing a strike!

CAN YOU SPOT:

THE BEST BEDROOM EVER

Every night, Gru tucks the girls into bed and reads Agnes a bedtime story. Their room is filled with fun things. Don't you wish your room were this awesome?!

CAN YOU SPOT:

WELCOME TO FREEDONIA!

Gru, Lucy, and the girls (and Jerry and Dave) go to Freedonia to meet Gru's long-lost twin brother, Dru! It turns out the family business is (can you guess?) pig farming!

CAN YOU SPOT:

FREEDONIA CHEESE FESTIVAL

Gru and Dru want to spend some together time on their own. So Lucy takes the girls out for a day of fun...at the local cheese festival! They have singing and dancing and...cheese jewelry? (Do you wear it or eat it?)

CAN YOU SPOT:

GET THAT PIZZA!

The Minions are *sooooooo* hungry. But they don't have jobs, and they don't have money, and their tiny, yellow tummies keep growling. What's that smell? A pizza delivery boy! Get him!

CAN YOU SPOT:

SING A SONG, MINIONS!

In the middle of the chase, the Minions end up on the stage of a popular talent show. Do they have what it takes to impress the judges and the fans? Or will the cops get them first?

CAN YOU SPOT:

SECURITY 45

BAD-BOY BLUES

Some of the Minions went to jail. But it's not fun at all, so they have to try to make their own fun. They soon realize they miss Gru and the outside world. Looks like being bad wasn't worth it! Crime doesn't pay.

CAN YOU SPOT:

The End? Nope!

We have a few more things hidden for you. Go back for another look and see if you can spot these extra-fun things.

CAN YOU SPOT:
an oyster with a pearl

CAN YOU SPOT:
parachuting pizza

CAN YOU SPOT:
6 pineapples

CAN YOU SPOT:
5 paper airplanes

CAN YOU SPOT:
a butterfly painting

CAN YOU SPOT:
propeller hat

CAN YOU SPOT:
boy wearing pig nose

CAN YOU SPOT:
fire hydrant

CAN YOU SPOT:
juggling Minion

CAN YOU SPOT:
cupcake